PRAISE FOR N

A fabulous soaring thriller.

— *TAKE OVER AT MIDNIGHT,* MIDWEST
BOOK REVIEW

Meticulously researched, hard-hitting, and suspenseful.

— *PURE HEAT,* PUBLISHERS WEEKLY,
STARRED REVIEW

Expert technical details abound, as do realistic military missions with superb imagery that will have readers feeling as if they are right there in the midst and on the edges of their seats.

— *LIGHT UP THE NIGHT,* RT REVIEWS, 4
1/2 STARS

Buchman has catapulted his way to the top tier of my favorite authors.

— FRESH FICTION

Nonstop action that will keep readers on the edge of their seats.

— *TAKE OVER AT MIDNIGHT,* LIBRARY JOURNAL

M L. Buchman's ability to keep the reader right in the middle of the action is amazing.

— LONG AND SHORT REVIEWS

The only thing you'll ask yourself is, "When does the next one come out?"

— *WAIT UNTIL MIDNIGHT,* RT REVIEWS, 4 STARS

The first...of (a) stellar, long-running (military) romantic suspense series.

— *THE NIGHT IS MINE,* BOOKLIST, "THE 20 BEST ROMANTIC SUSPENSE NOVELS: MODERN MASTERPIECES"

I knew the books would be good, but I didn't realize how good.

— NIGHT STALKERS SERIES, KIRKUS REVIEWS

Buchman mixes adrenalin-spiking battles and brusque military jargon with a sensitive approach.

13 times "Top Pick of the Month"

Tom Clancy fans open to a strong female lead will clamor for more.

Superb! Miranda is utterly compelling!

Miranda Chase continues to astound and charm.

Escape Rating: A. Five Stars! OMG just start with *Drone* and be prepared for a fantastic binge-read!

The best military thriller I've read in a very long time. Love the female characters.

A VERY JEREMY CHRISTMAS

A HOMECOMING CHRISTMAS STORY

M. L. BUCHMAN

SIGN UP FOR M. L. BUCHMAN'S NEWSLETTER TODAY

and receive:
Release News
Free Short Stories
a Free Book

Get your free book today. Do it now.
free-book.mlbuchman.com

Other works by M. L. Buchman: (* - also in audio)

Action-Adventure Thrillers

Dead Chef
One Chef!
Two Chef!

Miranda Chase
Drone*
Thunderbolt*
Condor*
Ghostrider*
Raider*
Chinook*
Havoc*
White Top*
Start the Chase*

Science Fiction / Fantasy

Deities Anonymous
Cookbook from Hell: Reheated
Saviors 101

Single Titles
Monk's Maze
the Me and Elsie Chronicles

Contemporary Romance

Eagle Cove
Return to Eagle Cove
Recipe for Eagle Cove
Longing for Eagle Cove
Keepsake for Eagle Cove

Love Abroad
Heart of the Cotswolds: England
Path of Love: Cinque Terre, Italy

Where Dreams
Where Dreams are Born
Where Dreams Reside
Where Dreams Are of Christmas*
Where Dreams Unfold
Where Dreams Are Written
Where Dreams Continue

Non-Fiction

Strategies for Success
Managing Your Inner Artist/Writer
Estate Planning for Authors*
Character Voice
Narrate and Record Your Own
Audiobook*

Short Story Series by M. L. Buchman:

Action-Adventure Thrillers

Dead Chef
Miranda Chase Origin Stories

Romantic Suspense

Antarctic Ice Fliers
US Coast Guard

Contemporary Romance

Eagle Cove

Other

Deities Anonymous (fantasy)
Single Titles

The Emily Beale Universe
(military romantic suspense)

The Night Stalkers
MAIN FLIGHT
The Night Is Mine
I Own the Dawn
Wait Until Dark
Take Over at Midnight
Light Up the Night
Bring On the Dusk
By Break of Day
Target of the Heart
Target Lock on Love
Target of Mine
Target of One's Own
NIGHT STALKERS HOLIDAYS
*Daniel's Christmas**
*Frank's Independence Day**
*Peter's Christmas**
Christmas at Steel Beach
*Zachary's Christmas**
*Roy's Independence Day**
*Damien's Christmas**
Christmas at Peleliu Cove

Henderson's Ranch
*Nathan's Big Sky**
*Big Sky, Loyal Heart**
*Big Sky Dog Whisperer**
*Tales of Henderson's Ranch**

Shadow Force: Psi
*At the Slightest Sound**
*At the Quietest Word**
*At the Merest Glance**
*At the Clearest Sensation**

White House Protection Force
*Off the Leash**
*On Your Mark**
*In the Weeds**

Firehawks
Pure Heat
Full Blaze
*Hot Point**
*Flash of Fire**
Wild Fire
SMOKEJUMPERS
*Wildfire at Dawn**
*Wildfire at Larch Creek**
*Wildfire on the Skagit**

Delta Force
*Target Engaged**
*Heart Strike**
*Wild Justice**
*Midnight Trust**

Emily Beale Universe Short Story Series
The Night Stalkers
The Night Stalkers Stories
The Night Stalkers CSAR
The Night Stalkers Wedding Stories
The Future Night Stalkers

Delta Force
Th Delta Force Shooters
The Delta Force Warriors

Firehawks
The Firehawks Lookouts
The Firehawks Hotshots
The Firebirds

White House Protection Force
Stories

Future Night Stalkers
Stories (Science Fiction)

ABOUT THIS BOOK

A MICROSOFT KID RAISED IN THE PACIFIC NORTHWEST, Jeremy had expected to follow in his family's footsteps, until he crossed a line he could never admit to.

He has found his place as an air-crash investigator for the NTSB, but coming home for Christmas threatens his place in his own family.

Coming back home and introducing his girlfriend to his family only makes it ten times more likely to be a disaster.

If he could have any wish for Christmas…

1

"You've got to be kidding me!"

"I do?" Jeremy Trahn, ever the straight man, was taking her literally.

Taz slumped in the passenger seat of his Prius Hybrid. She wasn't a slumping sort of person but going to meet Jeremy's parents for the first time—at Christmas— left her with few other options.

"What am I kidding you about?"

"You grew up out here in the woods?" They had driven from the team's shared house at the south end of Puget Sound, Washington, through the foreign land of Redmond and Microsoft, before falling off the edge of the earth. In the last few miles they'd rolled out the back of the chichi little city, gone through suburbia, and were now on a narrow one-lane road thick with trees and the occasional massive house. Most were bigger than the one that housed Miranda's entire air-crash investigation team.

"No, I grew up on Ames Lake."

She opened her mouth to ask, but closed it when she

caught a glimpse of a lake through the thick Douglas fir woods. Tangles of blackberry, alder, and wild rose cluttered the forest floor as it did in so much of the Pacific Northwest, but a driveway gap had offered a peek of the water far below.

Jeremy twisted onto an even narrower road that descended the bank toward the water.

"You aren't going to do anything stupid, are you, Jeremy?"

"It's me, so probably. What did you have in mind?"

One of the things she liked most about Jeremy was that he was almost impossible to offend. Which was a good thing given her own, frequently caustic nature. He was almost as emotionally tone deaf as Miranda's autism made her. Around the team, Taz's sniping remarks were unintentional, but that didn't stop them leaking out at awkward moments. It was also a weapon she'd wielded ruthlessly for nineteen years in the Pentagon and now used in the team's defense, which was probably all that kept her out of the *complete bitch* category.

Taz took a deep breath before confronting the problem head-on. "I know you, you plot out everything way ahead of time. You're not planning on proposing to me in front of your family or anything stupid like that, right?"

Jeremy spun to look at her in shock. "Am I supposed to? I didn't know that. How was I supposed to know that?"

Anyone else would be joking. And if they'd been traveling at any speed above Jeremy's careful adherence to the ten-mile-per-hour speed limit, they'd probably be in the ditch.

"I didn't plan anything. I haven't written a proposal. Or even started composing one. I'd need to look online and see how others did it before I could even know where to start. And I don't have a ring or anyth—"

"No, Jeremy," she cut him off which was about the only way to stop his rambling once he started. "You're *not* supposed to. I can't imagine ever being married. I just wanted to make sure that you weren't going to do something like that."

"Uh, no. I guess I wasn't. Mostly because I hadn't thought of it."

Well, that much was a relief.

"Never?" he asked, in one of his shortest comments ever, as he picked their way past mansion after mansion. A multi-story log monster like in the cedar home brochures only bigger. A tasteless thing that looked like a tract house on some combination of steroids for size and LSD for how many stupid porches, gables, terraces, and outbuildings had been tacked on in a failed attempt to mask its box-dull design. A sleek modernist glassy thing that let her see the lake straight through their living room and bedroom—life on tacky display.

"Let's see, Jeremy. Dad was a drug runner beheaded on the street in front of our Mexico City apartment. Mama was gunned down in a San Diego grocery store during a robbery. My former commanding US Air Force general declared a personal war on Mexico's cartel leaders because of his wife's death. No. I'm never getting married. So don't ever propose."

"Okay." And she could see Jeremy filing it away in that

neatly ordered mind of his. No way to read his reaction when he did that.

Another tacky McMansion. Then a small house no bigger than four rooms perched before a magnificent view; a holdout from before all the rest of the money had poured into the neighborhood. Its north-side roof slope was thick with green moss testifying to its age in place and how little the owners cared for appearances. She was disappointed when they rolled past. It was the only house she'd seen here that seemed halfway to normal.

Jeremy kept driving them downslope, south along the west side of the lake. The sunset views were shining through to either side of luxury homes. The woods upslope were thick, masking these homes from others above. Each was buffered from the next by manicured slices of privacy woods along the lot lines. He'd grown up with this as normal? Could their worldviews have been shaped more differently?

Her early life had been in barrios. Then decades that were mostly Air Force housing near her posting at the Pentagon. Now she lived in the team's house, in the heart of Gig Harbor. A town so small that everything was easily walkable—unlike anywhere else she'd ever lived.

Here was even stranger. These vast homes, each on their quarter- or half-acre lot, were either very private or terribly ostentatious. Or both.

"What do these places cost?"

"I dunno. Never really thought about it. A couple million, I guess."

Taz couldn't comprehend it. Or maybe she could. Their team leader *owned* one of the smaller San Juan

Islands in northern Puget Sound. She lived on it alone, in her big house that had once been a fishing and hunting resort. She also bought a four-million-dollar helicopter without batting an eye. Though she was no longer alone there since she'd hooked up with Andi.

Taz knew that Jeremy's parents had been with Microsoft since graduating college in the early nineties. Most of thirty years there, they were very high up in rank, so the cost of their home shouldn't be surprising—they were probably Microsoft millionaires several times over. But she still didn't know what to think about it.

She'd made good money by the time she'd climbed up to being an Air Force colonel and she'd banked most of it. She might be able to buy a home here—the small, run-down one—but it would tap her dry and she wouldn't be able to afford living here on what the National Transportation Safety Board paid her as a crash investigator.

He turned into the driveway of one of the nicest houses she'd seen yet, not in disrepair but not ridiculous either. A one-story with a steep-sloped roof. The architecture didn't scream *Look at me!* like so many of the others. Built into the slope, it was almost unpretentious.

Today was the twenty-third. All she had to survive was: tonight, Christmas Eve, Christmas, and gone on the twenty-sixth. Maybe the night of the twenty-fifth. Yeah. Two days and two nights.

She could do this.

2

JEREMY WAS SO RELIEVED TO STOP THE CAR. IT WAS AS IF his body had forgotten more and more of how to drive the closer he drew to home. He should have taken the longer way through Maple Valley and Fall City. If he had, his arrival would still be eleven minutes in the future. But he hadn't, so he was already here.

Maybe it wasn't too late to backtrack.

But it was. The car motor was off. Mom would have heard the crunch of tires on the gravel driveway and sent Dad to greet them.

Though Jeremy lived only sixty miles away, he came home very rarely, and he'd certainly never brought a girl home. A woman. Taz was nine years older than he was, had been an Air Force colonel, and he'd *never* understood why she was with him.

Together they sat in silence and stared at the house. The evening breeze riffled through the treetops but didn't reach them down here.

Maybe they could drive away and go find a hotel. Or

go back to the Gig Harbor house. Miranda and Andi were up on Miranda's island—sharing a first quiet Christmas as a couple. He'd never seen that coming. Until a few months ago, Miranda had been almost a surrogate mother, his team leader, and the pinnacle of what he'd hoped to become some day at the NTSB—an investigation team leader himself even half as good as she was.

And then she'd started dating Andi. It was...he didn't know...confusing? She had climbed down from her unattainable heights as the perfect crash investigator interested in nothing else, and become... human. It wasn't a bad thing—not exactly. But a piece of his world had shifted strangely in that moment and he was just as glad they were not invited to the island this year.

Except that it would be a great escape from this.

Mike and Holly were in Hawaii on a beach. Maybe he and Taz should have gone as well. He wondered if Mike had won or lost their bet about getting Holly into a bikini. Jeremy's money was on Holly's firm *No!* She had stubborn down to a science, though Mike was tricky and often found a way around that much to everyone's surprise—especially Holly's.

And he himself was...here.

He offered a brief prayer for his phone to ring with an air-crash to investigate.

It didn't.

Instead, the front door opened and Dad waved.

"Too late to run?" he whispered it though their car doors were still closed.

Taz looked at him in surprise. "Really? But they're your parents."

Jeremy closed his eyes for a moment, but he could feel his father approaching and opened them again. "They are." He pushed open the car door and climbed out. "Hey, Dad!"

He didn't dread coming home exactly; he missed his them all.

But they still didn't understand why he hadn't joined the rest of the family at Microsoft. Just four years since college and his big sister Caroline—who was a year younger but an inch taller and insisted on the *big sister* moniker—was already in charge of one of the small but significant applications. Another four years and she'd probably be leading one of the big teams. They were always judging him about his choice to work for the NTSB. Grandma had been at Microsoft since almost its beginning in the mid-eighties.

But there was the piece of his past they could never know about.

Maybe Taz would distract them.

But she was still sitting in the car. He circled around to open her door. She looked at him like he was insane.

"I'm not leading you into the lion's den. They're really nice."

She climbed out of the car. "Then why are *you* so afraid of them?"

"I am?"

"Jeremy," she leaned in to whisper as his dad approached, "we both are."

"Oh." Jeremy turned in time to hug Dad. It felt

normal. Was he afraid of his own father? He couldn't tell. Maybe afraid wasn't the right word. But if it wasn't, he had no idea what was.

However, Taz was usually right about such things. Not good.

3

——————

"AND YOU MUST BE THE ELUSIVE VICKI CORTEZ." JEREMY'S father was five-six to his son's five-seven, graying at the temples. Almost identical Vietnamese features.

Taz solved Thao Trahn's lack of appropriate next steps by offering her hand. He shook it.

"Taz. Everyone calls me Taz." He was still way above her own four-eleven. The tiny Mexican misfit. She'd never much belonged anywhere. But *definitely* didn't belong here in the land of Microsoft millionaires by any stretch of the imagination.

"Welcome and come on in," he snagged her daypack from the backseat before she could herself. It held a change of clothes and a toothbrush. Jeremy's pack had little more, and a cloth bag of presents that he'd asked for no help picking out.

Taz took a deep breath and followed him along the slate path from the graveled driveway to the front door.

The house was sided in age-darkened wood shingle

and topped with a green metal roof. A large wreath hung from the door with pinecones and a red ribbon.

Christmas for her had always been the Pentagon's standard departmental Christmas party—at which she'd never been drunk, disorderly, photocopied her ass, or fucked in the supplies closet. Christmas Day was a couple good action flicks and Chinese take-out from Mala Tang.

Jeremy had talked a lot about last Christmas up on Miranda's island.

Taz was relieved that it wasn't happening this year. She liked Miranda and Andi, but they were so...soft. That wasn't the right word. Pleasant? Whatever they were, the two women should be here, not her. A heavy dose of attitude was one of the things she shared with Holly. But women who were five-ten, beautiful, and spoke with a teasing Australian accent could get away with all kinds of shit that short-feisty Latinas couldn't pull off. She was thirty-five and still got carded in bars.

The outside of the house hadn't prepared her for the vast space within.

The deep great room was utterly dominated by the sweeping vista that looked along the length of the mile-long lake through towering windows. It was filled with the reds and golds of the western sky. Other houses were mere suggestions tucked into trees on the opposite shore.

Close by the glass, a broad terrace and the drop to the lawn indicated that it was a two-story house toward the lake side. By the water was a sitting area complete with a barbeque and outdoor kitchen setup. The short dock extended past a small boathouse appropriate for canoes or kayaks.

The high-vaulted, wood-lined room itself was a vast living and dining area combined. A gourmet kitchen filled the far end and an open door beyond revealed what must be a master suite. A partial loft above looked to be an open office space with several desks that still took advantage of the view. A carpeted stairway leading down indicated that there was indeed a story below. A pair of pure silver-gray cats inspected her from their perches on the back of the sofa.

Two slim elegant Vietnamese women, clearly mother and daughter, crossed over the parquet floor from the kitchen to greet them.

Taz considered how fast she could run in the other direction. Jeremy had the car keys. His father had her pack. Since when had she become so complacent that she didn't keep at *least* five thousand dollars of bugout money on her person at all times?

Shit! She had to fix that right away—if she survived this. She was losing her edge already.

When his mom offered a hug and Taz held out a hand, Caroline offered a sisterly smirk. Taz gave in and let herself be hugged. Other than Jeremy, she still wasn't comfortable being touched. Never had been.

Mai's hug was *not* perfunctory but was a wholehearted embrace that showed no signs of easing.

"I'm so glad he finally brought home a girl," she whispered in Taz's ear, clenching tighter. "I was giving up hope."

Maybe Taz could borrow a kitchen knife to throw herself on.

4

"Go rescue your girl, boy."

Jeremy jumped as his grandmother stepped up beside him. She'd always been a stealth grandma, appearing by transporter beam. Which was a good trick as she was a tall woman with radiantly blonde hair.

"Now!" she gave him a push toward Taz before he could hug her.

"Hey, Mom," Jeremy stepped over. "Can I have a hug?"

It didn't go quite as he'd planned, Mom freed up one arm so that she was hugging them both. Caroline leaned in to rap her knuckles sharply on his head—her idea of a laugh-riot joke. As normal, he was in no position to retaliate.

"Hey! Ow!" His flinch finally broke up Mom's bear hug. She might be little taller than Taz but she had a powerful grip.

Mom gave Taz a final squeeze.

When Jeremy started to put an arm around Taz's

shoulder, she got that look that said if he did, he'd be getting his arm back in three or four pieces. He kept it to himself.

"And this," he turned her attention without quite touching her, "is my grandma, Amy Collins."

Taz remained frozen in place staring at Grandma wide-eyed.

"Warn her next time, boy," Grandma patted Jeremy's cheek, then took Taz's limp hand and shook it. "Hi. Yes, I'm a blonde Caucasian. And yes, Mai is my daughter. Barry, bless his soul, and I adopted her when she was part of Operation Babylift at the end of the Vietnam War. And yes, Mai has always been very clingy. Any other immediate questions?"

Taz shook her head slowly.

"Maybe I should get a t-shirt made that answers those questions up front. What do you think?"

Taz nodded. Then shook her head. Then shuddered like a cat trying to shed water sprinkled on its coat. "Skip the t-shirt. But I think you should give some lessons to your grandson, very soon."

Grandma Amy laughed. "I suspect that I can leave that up to you, but we'll see."

Jeremy felt a tickle at his neck, but was able to spin fast enough to stop Caroline putting an ice cube down his back. Instead she dropped it down the front of his turtleneck. "Caro!" Caroline absolutely wasn't sweet like the Karo corn syrup which had prompted her nickname.

"Be glad it wasn't a holly branch. They're very prickly."

He contemplated vengeance, but that was always a dangerous challenge with his sister. He should have said, *You mean* you're *very prickly.* But the moment had passed. He always thought of good comebacks too late.

5

TAZ WAS, GOD HELP HER, CRAWLING INTO THE BACK SEAT OF the family minivan. Not a familiar military-huge Chevy Suburban with tinted glass, but a Toyota Sienna seven-passenger civilian rig. With all of the gewgaws, of course. Dashcam, digital rearview mirror offering an unobstructed view, fold-down-from-the-ceiling entertainment system for the rear passengers (including a collection of wireless headphones), hybrid drive, and probably seventy-three other computerized systems she didn't know about.

It was weirdly Middle America—the happy family all heading off together in a piece of Japanese-designed luxury Americana.

Father and grandmother in front. Mother and sister in the middle. And she and Jeremy tucked into the back because they were the *young* couple.

That she was the half generation between Jeremy and his parents was decidedly odd. She already didn't belong for so many reasons. Yet Mai had clung to her like she was a savior rather than a pariah. Prior to this year, she'd always embodied the pariah role. Certainly, her nineteen years at the Pentagon hadn't made her anyone's idea of a good companion. She'd personally delivered the hammer blow of three-star General Martinez's wishes to military and contractors alike.

Yet Jeremy's sweetness had slipped past all of her guards. And somehow that had led her to an impossible world, which placed her in the backseat of a freaking minivan bound for an unknown annual Christmas ritual.

The chatter among the four of them was hard to follow, all about the various projects and personalities at Microsoft. She'd always been able to read a room; it was one of her specialties. It was easier to take control of a group once the dynamics were understood.

But the more she listened to the Trahns and Grandma Collins, only just retiring now, the more Taz heard the mysterious stuff that lay underneath the surface in this group.

It wasn't the career.

It wasn't merely the past.

They were close. Family close. It was a sound she hadn't heard in the decades between Mama's death and joining Miranda's air-crash investigation team. The exposure was like a chill winter storm—they were family, she wasn't.

In her early days with Miranda, each time she joined a non-work-related conversation it had crashed and died as surely as the worst plane disaster. It was getting better now. In the last months she'd become an asset to the team, no longer an untrusted outsider. She'd also been living with Jeremy the entire time.

Four months now they'd been doing that. She'd never lived with a man. And, except for moments like the present, it oddly kept being easy. And good! Which even stranger than easy. She *was* getting soft. Jeremy was being a bad influence.

The few miles to their destination passed quickly and soon the were climbing from the van. The mid-winter darkness made the minivan's boxy shape and Celestial Silver Metallic finish look like a modernistic WWII Sherman tank. All it needed was the gun turret and a set of big steel tracks.

Was she at war?

If so, she had no idea who the enemy was this time.

6

THEY JOINED THE FLOW OF OTHER FAMILIES WALKING UP the hill from the lower parking lot. People's gestures were brisk in the cold snap of the air, but their progress was slow as it was a family outing. Jeremy kept a strong hold of Taz's hand for support. She wasn't into holding hands, but his grip must have transmitted some degree of his desperation as she didn't shake him off. They strolled up the slope of the tree-bordered sidewalk along Main Street,

He could feel the hidden message lurking within every one of his family's Microsoft stories. *You could be part of this. Why aren't you? Why do you visit so rarely? Why do you* hate *our lives?* Even his sister's tone kept asking why he was judging them.

He wasn't—but he couldn't explain. He'd crossed too many ethical and legal lines back in his brief foray as a teenage hacker. The acceptable answer had been to leave. His transgression was hidden, unknown, but he couldn't risk it coming back to haunt his family.

Besides, now he had a place with Miranda's team that he wouldn't trade for the world. And for only the second time in his life he had a girlfriend.

And one he was living with? That was impossibly new and wonderful...except that moment before he came fully awake each morning wondering if Taz would still be there beside him. Or would she be untraceably gone from his life? He didn't know if that was a stupid fear or not, but at the moment he was desperately glad to have her at his side as they followed the path toward the Bellevue Botanic Garden.

He'd never missed a year of their Garden d'Lights since its founding, though he'd attended the first one somewhere between conception and birth. Every December 23rd the Collins and the Trahns had come here. And now Taz was part of the family tradition. Would she be here for the next year and the one after that?

Oh, was that why he wasn't supposed to propose, because she wouldn't be? No, she'd said never, which didn't make any sense.

Was his family asking the same question? Expecting that? Maybe they were, and he finally understood quite what he had hauled her into.

"Hey, Taz. Are you okay with this?" he whispered.

"Sure, why not?" It sounded as if her teeth were clenched.

"Seriously? You don't sound sure."

"I'm fine. Just don't let go or I might explode." She clamped his hand tightly enough in hers that he wondered how much it would hurt when she let go and the blood flow returned.

"That goes both ways. Promise you won't let go."

"Okay. Though you better explain that some day."

"Yeah, Jeremy," Caro took advantage of the slowdown at the ticket booth to clamp her hand around his other biceps. "What the hell is up with you?"

"Ow! Ease off, Caro." He shook his arm to no avail. He might be older by a year, but she was taller and very strong. She'd kept up with the martial arts he'd dropped when he'd left for college.

"You're sitting on something, Jeremy. Don't make me beat it out of you. You know I can."

He knew it. "Not now, Caro. Okay? Can't we just enjoy the lights?" Jeremy nodded toward Grandma and their parents leading the way.

She shrugged a maybe, barely visible through her winter coat, offered a final crushing squeeze, then let him loose.

Taz's grip had only tightened.

"Let's look at the lights, okay?"

She nodded, but didn't ease up.

7

TAZ COULD FEEL JEREMY THINKING JEREMY THOUGHTS. He'd tossed her into the middle of a family ritual. Like she'd be here forever now.

Oh Christ! He *had* thought about happily ever after— with her! In that case she'd have to kill him and bury him. There must be a dark corner somewhere among the brilliant lights.

Yet he had also thought that he should find out if she was okay. That was a major advance for Jeremy.

The lights. Look at the lights. Focus.

The entry was a grand arch of white twinkle lights, offering mere glimpses of the multi-colored wonders beyond.

"Here's a map," Mai handed it to her. "The challenge is to find each type of animal and the new plants too. You and Jeremy go ahead, dear. I promise not to hover." Then she offered a self-deprecating smile. "At least as much as I can help. This was always Jeremy's favorite part of the season and I don't know what happened. One year it was a wonder and the next I felt as if I was dragging him here in chains to—"

"Standing right here, Mom."

"Of course you are, dear. I never said you weren't. Well, you youngsters go on ahead." And she gave them a small shove forward.

There was no question where Jeremy had gotten his ability to reel out long cascades of words. In fact, an unusual reticence had kicked in as soon as they'd turned into his family's driveway. Maybe he really was as nervous to come home as he'd suggested in the car.

Taz tried to figure out why as they shuffled forward with the crowd.

Except the sight was so breathtaking that she could only stare. Tiny Christmas lights in every color had been shaped into sculptures. A green rose bush with face-sized red roses stood directly in front of them. At its feet was a small pool of blue lights. In it floated a green light lily pad and on that perched a foot-long ladybug in shining red with black gaps for its spots and face, each outlined in darkest purple. A story-tall willow tree sprouted before them in fragile tendrils of green dripping from a beige trunk.

Everywhere she looked there was a new shape revealed in glowing Christmas colors. Each refocusing revealed more fanciful light sculptures.

"There are over a half-million bulbs here. The volunteers spend thousands of hours designing and installing these each year. They've been adding to the original display of a set of grape vines for most of three decades."

Taz couldn't look away to glance at Jeremy. Every time she tried there was something else to see. Little girls and boys stood at the light chain marking the border of the walkway, pointing with exclamations of joy as they identified one thing or another. Parents weren't looking indulgent; they were looking fascinated in their own right.

Two decades in Washington, D.C. hadn't made her forget her first fifteen years. She was mostly aghast at such a display. These people had no idea how good they had it compared to her youth in the Mexico City and San Diego barrios.

And yet, she herself couldn't stop looking at the lights in wonder. There was too much joy here to ignore.

"Oh look at the rabbit," Jeremy's voice echoed his own wonder. It was squatting under a brown and green palm tree next to a patch of what must be lettuce.

And in that instant, he...shifted. When they'd first met so briefly, he'd been an innocent in so many ways. Not simple, but naive. And he'd had a positivity that poured out of him. It had drawn her in ways that she was only seeing now.

And coming here to his parents for Christmas, with her along, had spun him into a hole so deep she almost didn't recognize him. Had she taken all the light out of him?

These last months he'd become so much more serious. Was she bad for Jeremy?

Had he started hiding within his work? No, that intense focus was always him. To be more dedicated, he'd have to become like Miranda and even she was loosening up...well, a tiny bit. Which was a lot for her.

Was Taz herself the one who had knocked that joy out of him? It sounded likely. She was the only other variable, wasn't she?

Or was it going to see his family?

He'd been unusually quiet on the drive up. Had told her almost nothing about them or their home—not that she'd asked. The last of her family was twenty-five years in the grave and such thoughts simply weren't on her radar. But still, like his grandmother had said, he should have forewarned her.

They strolled past a forest of sunflowers towering twice her height, too artfully done to see the wire that must be holding them aloft.

Next was a broad lake of bright blue ten or fifteen meters across. She'd always found that color of Christmas lights to be sad, but it was impossible to feel that about this scene. In the middle of the fanciful lake were white swans and gold-and-brown ducks. The lake shore boasted bountiful flowers in twenty or more varieties of which she only recognized a few. And so much more. Swallow houses were lit with Christmas cheer, and birds on the wing were suspended impossibly in the air to shine their lights.

If she was the reason Jeremy had lost his joy, she was gone. Yes, it would mean leaving another team. Even if it meant hurting Jeremy. He was too important for her to damage.

When she went to wipe her face with her hands, one

of them was still stuck in Jeremy's grasp. She tried to tug it free.

"Nuh-uh. You promised." Jeremy kept his hold on her.

"I promised what?"

"To not let go."

They stood on the shores of the light lake, a flock of waist-high children giggling and pointing in a swarm around them.

"Are you sure keeping me around is a good thing?" She hadn't meant to blurt it out like that but she wasn't practiced about discussing her own feelings.

"With my parents here? I can't keep you close enough."

Taz had to consider that long enough that they began following the shore as the tide of children swept them forward.

"So, I'm a distraction for your parents."

"Yeah. That sounds good. Anything to keep them distracted."

"And if not me, you'd have brought one of the others."

Jeremy shook his head. "No, two are in Hawaii. And Andi and Miranda said *no* when I invited them."

"They want to be alone together. They're trying on a new relationship. You know that."

Jeremy stopped them in front of a trio of arm-span long fishes that were in mid-leap out of the blue lake light. But he didn't say anything. It felt as if he was embarrassed by her but she knew it wasn't that. Or it certainly hadn't been before today.

"Jeremy. Why am I here?" She didn't have any more clue than these fake fish caught in mid-leap.

"I just need someone—"

"There you are," Mai exclaimed as the rest of the family plowed into them. "Enough time together. We want to get to know your girl, Jeremy. You men go ahead." She flapped a hand at Jeremy and his dad.

Jeremy sent her a pleading look as their hands were pulled apart. A look that she had no way to interpret because she was the one who'd just been thrown into the deep end.

So she *was* here only as a distraction. Not as a girlfriend to be introduced to his family. He was going to pay for that one in blood.

8

HE AND DAD HAD DONE AS THEY ALWAYS DID, TALKED about the code behind *Flight Simulator,* the product team his dad had headed for Microsoft for years. They talked about how to emulate on-screen the complex aircraft that Jeremy studied in real life—at least the ones that had crashed.

With the help of the excited children flocking about them, they found the snail, the turtle, and tomatoes. Jeremy dutifully checked them off on the tour map, including the ones he'd been unable to check off while holding Taz's hand.

They stopped to admire the work of the new giant web and spider.

The women hustled by them at that point, with Caro offering a clear, "Eww! Creepy."

He tried to catch Taz's eye, but when he did, all he got in turn was a scowl. It was one of her dangerous, I'm-about-to-kill-someone looks and it was aimed at him. At least he thought that's what it was. He'd never been good at guessing what she was thinking. Asking had been the answer to that, but getting her alone since the moment they'd pulled up to the house hadn't been easy. Or possible at all.

Jeremy barely remembered the rest of the walk, though he saw by the critter map he still clutched at the exit that they'd checked off every item on the list. He couldn't even recall seeing his perennial favorite, the long green dragon arcing out of the ground in grand sinuous loops as if it could swim through the earth itself. Missing the dragon was like missing a piece of himself.

But it was too late to double back. He'd ended up in the van's middle seat with Mom who was squeezing the life out of his one hand as hard as Taz had been squeezing the other. Taz and Caro were in the way back seat, but their whispers were drowned out by Mom's family news that covered a hundred topics, each for only an eyeblink or two.

Back at the house, after the traditional post-Garden d'Lights hot cocoa, they were in his room. Finally.

"What the—" Jeremy could only stare. Mom had changed out the old twin bed with a double, probably in the last forty-eight hours since he'd said he was bringing Taz home. He'd never had a girl here before, and now his room was changed. Different. For years it was always the same every time. And now—

"Keys," Taz held out her hand.

Jeremy reached into his pocket for the car keys. "Did you leave something in the car?"

Her look was grim as she continued to hold out her hand without saying a word.

And he knew, he somehow simply *knew,* that if she got her hands on them, she'd be gone and he'd be waking up alone for a long time to come. It was only then that he noticed she'd shouldered her daypack.

He kept his hand clenched so tightly around the keys that they cut into his palm.

"No." He'd never argued with Taz before and he wasn't sure what would happen next.

Apparently neither was Taz as she remained with her hand out for a long moment before slowly closing her fingers. "Jeremy. I need to not be here."

"Why?"

Her growl was low and dangerous. "You don't want me to answer that. Now give me the keys. Don't make me walk. I will."

"Actually, if you walk, I'll go with you. And I *do* want you to answer why you want to leave." He sat down on the edge of his new bed to prove his point.

"Because, asshole, you only want me here as a buffer to your family."

"No I don't."

"It's what you said, Jeremy. Don't lie. Are you even capable of lying?"

He felt the knife go in. She didn't know. She couldn't know. He'd done nothing but lie to his family since the summer after high school. He dug out the keys and threw them at her.

Taz snatched them from mid-air.

"Fine. Go. Just don't ask!" And he closed his eyes so that he didn't have to watch her walk out of his life.

But he didn't hear her go. No shuffling step on the carpet. No door opening then closing forever behind her. Not even the squeak from the middle hinge that he'd never been able to fix as a kid. Nothing he could fix anymore anyway.

9

Taz massaged the keys with her thumb. Every instinct said this wasn't her problem. They'd had a fun time and now it was over.

That had become the story of her life. The Pentagon career had died along with three-star General Martinez —she was supposed to die beside him, but hadn't. The one season as a wildland firefighter had been burned away when her past had caught up with her. And the last four months on Miranda's air-crash investigation team had just now crashed and burned.

Was that her future life? From one disaster to the next unholy trainwreck?

If she walked out the door, that's what it would be. Maybe for the rest of her days, however few those were.

But she couldn't turn. Jeremy sat on the edge of his bed with his head hung like he'd been beaten. She couldn't find the person inside her who, in the past, could have walked away from his misery without another thought.

She could face down entire project management teams or territory-defending generals for massive Air Force contracts. But that didn't tell her what to do next here.

"Jeremy?"

"Please go." And by the pain in his voice, she knew she couldn't.

Instead she sat on the edge of the bed beside him. Out the windows, she could see the quarter moon shimmering on the lake water. Lights of distant homes sparkled like Christmas lights along the far shore. How could it be so serene when she felt as if her guts were a coiled wire about to detonate her life.

"I don't want to talk about it."

And that was her key. What if all this wasn't about her but about him? She'd asked if he was afraid of his family. He'd said no. And he clearly loved them. But he also worried them.

There was no way to approach it directly. She expected that her normal battering-ram technique would only throw his defenses up even higher. So, she'd try coming at him sideways.

"Why am I here, Jeremy? And I'm warning you ahead of time, if your answer is that I'm just a buffer, a distraction to keep you from interacting with your family, I'm so fucking gone."

"You're just—" he started far too quickly.

"Without lying!"

He clenched his jaw and hung his head even further.

She let the silence stretch.

"Isn't it what I'm supposed to do?" He finally offered softly.

"What?"

"Bring the woman I love home to meet my family?"

"The woman you love?" Why did men use that word so easily?

"Since the first time we met—"

"When I kidnapped you and Mike."

"Right. I haven't thought of another woman since then. You're so alive and different. So unlike anyone I've ever met. I'm braver just by trying to be more like you. I'm...better around you. Do you know what that's like? To want someone to appreciate you more, so you strive to become your best self around them? Miranda makes me do that and so do you. And you like me despite my being...me."

"Everyone likes you, Jeremy. You're likeable. Own it. *I'm* the heartless bitch." Which she owned far too readily.

"Well they shouldn't like me. They wouldn't if they knew." And again he collapsed into silence.

Maybe this really wasn't about her at all. Though they definitely had to have it out over that *woman I love* comment, maybe this wasn't the time. She opened her mouth and closed it again. Her main weapon was words and she'd been about to apply them with her usual subtlety of a crowbar. If she did, she might wound Jeremy as thoughtlessly as she had so many others in her lengthy career as an enforcer for her general.

"I wasn't always..." Jeremy started, then his words drifted away.

"...such a good person." She finished for him, yet he

41

was. The best she'd ever been with. Perhaps the best she'd ever met. Maybe walking away from him wasn't one of her better ideas.

"Yeah. That."

"That's hard to imagine, Jeremy."

"It's true. There are only two people who know. One has retired to Lithuania. And Holly."

"Holly?"

"Well, she only knows part of it, but she promised not to tell. I made her promise."

Taz took both of Jeremy's hands in hers and braced herself. It wasn't a fair tactics because she knew what buttons to push on Jeremy. They were so obvious on him that it was child's play. She just hoped that she didn't hate herself for using it afterward.

"Okay, Jeremy look at me. Are you listening?"

He looked up and nodded.

"If you trust me, you have to tell me what happened."

10

IT WAS DURING CHRISTMAS EVE DINNER PREP THAT JEREMY finally found the nerve to tell his family. He'd asked Taz to keep the truth to herself for twenty-four hours, and those were going to run out tonight after dinner. To make sure he didn't chicken out, she'd threatened to tell them herself if he didn't. She was never subtle when she knew she was right. Something he usually appreciated about her.

Grandma had declared that the women were in the kitchen and the men should stay out of the way. That wasn't what usually happened on Christmas Eve and Jeremy could only assume that Taz was behind it. She'd joined in with the others, proving that she was a good hand in the kitchen.

She'd also agreed to make sure their few belongings were packed in case they had to leave on short notice.

He'd thought about taking Dad for a walk down to the lake. Or at least downstairs where they'd be alone together.

Instead, he knew it had to be where it had all started. He led his father up to the loft office overlooking the great room and the lake. As long as they didn't shout, their voices would be masked by the four women in the kitchen and the Christmas carols playing softly over the house sound system.

This is where it had all begun.

Four desks. All sported the latest Microsoft Surface machines.

"Your grandmother took over yours when you stopped coming home. Your sister sometimes still uses hers when she's visiting, like now."

How many hours had they all spent here in this loft. "A family that plays together, stays together." He whispered the family maxim.

His father looked infinitely sad. "It didn't work out so well, did it?" He rested a hand on Jeremy's shoulder.

Jeremy looked down at the gathering of women in the kitchen below and the sunset once again sweeping across the lake, lighting it gold, and reflecting the warm light up against the ceiling of the great room and loft.

"It wasn't your fault." He dropped into his grandmother's chair that had once been his.

"Then whose was it?" His father sat close by in his.

Jeremy wanted to hide his face. To scream. To…

He was always worried that Taz would run away from him, waking each morning to the fear of her not being there. Now, perhaps, he understood part of that impulse.

The only way forward, Taz had insisted last night, *was to face it.*

She'd had a very puzzled look on her face as she'd

said it, but she'd nodded to herself as if it was answering some other question at the same time.

"I did something really stupid, Dad. That summer before college, I was trying to impress a girl, so I stole one of your passwords." He took a deep breath for courage and didn't find any. But he was past stopping. "I engineered a hack through the Flight Simulator that you developed for the Air Force so that I could reach in through their supercomputers and, using data we scraped out of Boeing's design computers, I could take over a plane from the pilot—and fly it. I'm so sorry. I never meant any harm. I didn't let *her* do it. I caught myself before I let her. Or my boss did. Or maybe we both did. I don't even know. But I betrayed all of your trust in me and I just couldn't..."

He finally ran out of words. He'd broken his father's trust and had lied about it ever since.

His Dad was silent for a long time. He'd forgotten that about his father. Thao Trahn always thought things through very carefully before speaking. Jeremy wished he did too, but he was Mai's son. It was Caro who was their father's daughter.

"The girl? This one?" His father asked shortly before Jeremy was going to pass out from holding his breath.

"No, Dad. This was years ago. I've only known Taz since last winter."

"What happened?"

"Nothing bad. I turned a C-5 through twenty degrees and then back without the pilot noticing. That's all. Ever!" Which wasn't actually true, but the President had made it very clear that his second effort was on behalf of the nation and was top secret. It wasn't to be disclosed to anyone without his express permission. He'd thought about calling to ask for it, but that would mean interrupting Miranda's vacation with Andi to reach the President on Christmas Eve, and that would— Taz had vetoed the idea. She'd worked in the Pentagon, so he figured she'd know best.

"I meant what happened to the girl?"

He didn't think that was a secret...particularly. "She and two friends were caught by the FBI for that when they tried to override my security system. Then, it turned out, they'd colluded on a number of other hacks. Some really bad ones. Things neither I nor my boss ever knew about. They're going to be in prison for a long time yet."

His dad was silent again for so long that Jeremy wondered if his hearing still worked. Then he realized he could hear the women half singing along with "The Chipmunk Song" –*Christmas don't be late*—in high squeaky voices.

"You know your mother's and my history."

Jeremy nodded. Orphans loaded on some of the last flights to leave Vietnam at the end of the Vietnam War in 1974. No past. No parents. Scattered across the world, many in the US, but also elsewhere. Yet his parents had both ended up in Microsoft, met there, married, and had children.

"We came to a country defined by conflicts and contradictions. We escaped Vietnam and we lost our parents because the US and China decided to have a war about communism on our soil. Yet, we gained such a life because of Grandma and Grandpa Collins. Look where we live, Jeremy. Because of those conflicts and contradictions."

There was no questioning the opportunity or the luxury of where they were sitting.

"You cleaned up after yourself?"

"I erased everything. All the code." And he had, eventually. "Since then I trained myself to save every plane I could. I became the best crash investigator I knew how. People compare me to Miranda Chase, which is crazy because she's so amazing, but I try."

Dad stood, as if stretching his legs. After a long moment he patted Jeremy's shoulder. "You should come home more often. Your mother worries." And then he headed down the stairs to join the others.

11

Taz wasn't sure why, but Thao had sent her to the office loft. Not with words, just a nod of his head. She couldn't read his expression.

Angry father mode about to banish them both forever from the house?

Some mandate about her being a bad influence for reasons she couldn't imagine?

Some horrid penance Jeremy must pay for what he'd done?

She almost went downstairs first to grab their packs so that they could just run.

Screw that, just run anyway. She'd pocketed Jeremy's car keys from the top of the dresser in case they needed to make a fast getaway.

Taz eased up the spiral staircase to the loft and spotted Jeremy seated in the shadows: elbows on knees and head hanging down much like last night.

Not good. Definitely not good.

She stepped up to him. "Come on. Let's go. Let's get out of here."

He shook his head. Instead he reached out and snagged her hand to pull her against him. Head by her hip, he wrapped his arms around her waist, and simply held on.

Taz stroked his hair as he held onto her, not saying a word for a long time. It was a relief actually after all the words Mai had used while they were cooking. They'd ultimately bonded over how often they were both looking at the loft with worried expressions.

Knowing that Jeremy hadn't been avoiding his home because of her had been a start. Learning that he was using her as a distraction, became less and less annoying as she understood more of his fears.

Family had always been the most important thing to her: her mother, her first military mentor, and the sense of family from General Martinez.

But Jeremy came from a real family. Out of whatever breakage had occurred in the past, they had all been coming together for twenty-five years to go visit Christmas lights in the Bellevue Botanic Gardens. Did they understand how brightly they shone in comparison to her own past? To the world around them?

Hopefully not. Let them simply be who they were. Let this all be okay.

By comparison she'd never actually had family, not like this one. It was—

Jeremy sat up in his chair and looked up at her. His cheeks were wet, but he was smiling.

"I want you to know that I heard what you said."

"Which what? I've said a lot of things."

Jeremy nodded eagerly. "Which isn't like you. But they're good things. Mostly. There's one thing that you said wrong though and I figure that I'm going to have to change your mind on that. Not now. Because I promised. But—"

"Jeremy!" she cut off his torrent of words.

He sobered instantly, then reached out to slip his fingers into her hair and brush it over her shoulder, just as he had the very first time he'd ever touched her. They'd both been naked, she been about to use his body most happily, yet his first touch had been to simply brush at her hair.

And she saw that the sweet man who'd knocked her feet out from under her was still there.

He'd survived her, his past, and his father. Perhaps the growing seriousness that she'd observed was maturity, for how could a man go through all he had this last year and not be changed.

"Maybe next year," he kissed her on her ear and then whispered into it.

"Maybe next year what?"

"Maybe when we come here next Christmas, you'll let me propose to you."

"Not a chance!" Taz gave him her best scoff.

Next year.

At Christmas—Mama had always loved Christmas.

Maybe here, with Jeremy and his family, she would too.

Year after year?

Somehow, when she wasn't paying attention, Jeremy

had gotten around her defenses. Maybe not such a bad Christmas present after all.

———

If you enjoyed this story
please consider leaving a review.
They really help.

Keep reading for an exciting excerpt from:
White House Protection Force #1: *Off the Leash*

TWELVE TALES OF CHRISTMAS (EXCERPT)

IF YOU ENJOYED THAT, YOU'LL LOVE
THIS COLLECTION!

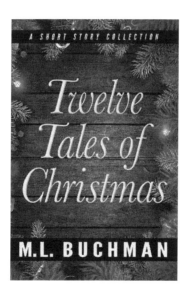

TWELVE TALES OF CHRISTMAS
(EXCERPT)

MASTER SERGEANT DUSTIN JAMES NUDGED A CLOD OF DIRT back into place with the toe of his boot. The rich black soil of the Portland Oregon Rose Garden simply dissolved and left a blackish patch of mud on the worn leather. Today was the Winter Solstice. It was raining and about three degrees above freezing. Pretty typical. He stared down at the *Rosa canina*.

This rose had been propagated from a cutting of the oldest documented rose bush on the planet. The rose now huddled, dormant and pruned back for the winter. In bloom, it was the least assuming rose in the garden, a single layer of five pink petals around a yellow center. Four days before Christmas, it was a cluster of frosty twigs decorated by bright red rose hips.

Most people passed it by, but not his father, the head gardener of the nearby Japanese Garden. He had visited the rose every day after work on his walk home. Dusty and his mother had often walked up to meet him at the old Briar Rose.

"I met your mother by this rose. We married right here." Being a man of few words, his father never embellished the story. It wasn't the most scenic spot in the garden, but with ten thousand rose bushes in a couple hundred neatly tended beds, not bad either. The fact that they'd married here on the Winter Solstice when nothing bloomed had been a little odd perhaps, but then his parents had been rather eccentric.

Dusty had come home for this Christmas, even though his parents had been gone for three years. Their small condo now lay empty most of the year due to a crashed tourist helicopter. An old Bell 206 called in an engine failure and then auto-rotated right into an Icelandic volcano, no survivors.

That Dusty was a crew chief and mechanic on a Sikorsky Black Hawk for the U.S. Army's 160th SOAR had made the loss beyond ironic. His job was to fly, fight, and keep the Special Operations Aviation Regiment choppers running perfectly despite war conditions. His parents had died, probably from a broken fan belt.

So, any time that he was home, but especially on the Winter Solstice, he made a point of coming to visit their rose as his parents had done so often for their three decades together.

"I'm glad you went together, at least you got that much," he told the sleeping rose. With no ashes to scatter, he'd gathered some ash from the volcano and scattered it onto the rose's soil. His parents belonged together here. His father, a quiet man who loved visiting the garden's roses, such a contrast to his artistic Japanese garden, and his wild mother, a true child of the sixties, who had never understood Dusty's choice to serve. They appeared such an oddly-matched couple, the slight Eurasian and the tall, busty blonde. "She brings me to life like the spring warmth." "He keeps me steady with his deep roots."

When would Dusty find that? His own dreams had just been pruned back hard. He'd found out, on no notice, that he had a week's leave. He'd rushed back to Portland only to discover that Nancy had meant to Dear Dusty him, but forgotten, as usual, to follow through. Another woman who hadn't understood his need to serve his country, his need to protect that which was so precious. She was living with some software geek named Ralph.

Dusty's few friends still in the area were busy with pre-holiday family stuff. Some invited him over for a meal, but being a third wheel in some other couple's holiday wasn't his first choice, nor his second or third.

On call, Dusty really didn't have time to go anywhere els—

The cry of pain echoing across the garden snapped him out of his damp reverie. His Special Forces training had him sprinting down the garden path before he even fully registered what was happening.

One hand slapped for his sidearm, and came away empty. The other slapped for the med kit on his SARVSO survival vest, but he wore only a rain slick over his heavy sweater.

The cry sounded again, a woman in agonizing pain. Halfway across the garden from his parents' rose, he spotted the source. Not that it was hard. On a rainy, winter Friday morning there was only one other person in the garden.

She knelt in the mud at the edge of a garden bed.

Dusty rushed up beside her. "Where are you hurt?" Seeing no obvious wounds he started unzipping her parka.

Her punch came out of nowhere.

————

Keep reading now!
12 great stories of romance and adventure
Available at fine retailers everywhere.
Twelve Tales of Christmas

ABOUT THE AUTHOR

USA Today and Amazon #1 Bestseller M. L. "Matt" Buchman has 70+ action-adventure thriller and military romance novels, 100 short stories, and lotsa audiobooks. PW says: "Tom Clancy fans open to a strong female lead will clamor for more." Booklist declared: "3X Top 10 of the Year." A project manager with a geophysics degree, he's designed and built houses, flown and jumped out of planes, solo-sailed a 50' sailboat, and bicycled solo around the world...and he quilts. More at: www.mlbuchman.com.

Other works by M. L. Buchman: (* - also in audio)

Action-Adventure Thrillers

Dead Chef
One Chef!
Two Chef!

Miranda Chase
*Drone**
*Thunderbolt**
*Condor**
*Ghostrider**
*Raider**
*Chinook**
*Havoc**
*White Top**
*Start the Chase**

Science Fiction / Fantasy

Deities Anonymous
Cookbook from Hell: Reheated
Saviors 101

Single Titles
Monk's Maze
the Me and Elsie Chronicles

Contemporary Romance

Eagle Cove
Return to Eagle Cove
Recipe for Eagle Cove
Longing for Eagle Cove
Keepsake for Eagle Cove

Love Abroad
Heart of the Cotswolds: England
Path of Love: Cinque Terre, Italy

Where Dreams
Where Dreams are Born
Where Dreams Reside
*Where Dreams Are of Christmas**
Where Dreams Unfold
Where Dreams Are Written
Where Dreams Continue

Non-Fiction

Strategies for Success
Managing Your Inner Artist/Writer
*Estate Planning for Authors**
Character Voice
Narrate and Record Your Own
*Audiobook**

Short Story Series by M. L. Buchman:

Action-Adventure Thrillers

Dead Chef

Miranda Chase Origin Stories

Romantic Suspense

Antarctic Ice Fliers

US Coast Guard

Contemporary Romance

Eagle Cove

Other

Deities Anonymous (fantasy)

Single Titles

The Emily Beale Universe
(military romantic suspense)

The Night Stalkers
MAIN FLIGHT
The Night Is Mine
I Own the Dawn
Wait Until Dark
Take Over at Midnight
Light Up the Night
Bring On the Dusk
By Break of Day
Target of the Heart
Target Lock on Love
Target of Mine
Target of One's Own
NIGHT STALKERS HOLIDAYS
Daniel's Christmas*
Frank's Independence Day*
Peter's Christmas*
Christmas at Steel Beach
Zachary's Christmas*
Roy's Independence Day*
Damien's Christmas*
Christmas at Peleliu Cove

Henderson's Ranch
Nathan's Big Sky*
Big Sky, Loyal Heart*
Big Sky Dog Whisperer*
Tales of Henderson's Ranch*

Shadow Force: Psi
At the Slightest Sound*
At the Quietest Word*
At the Merest Glance*
At the Clearest Sensation*

White House Protection Force
Off the Leash*
On Your Mark*
In the Weeds*

Firehawks
Pure Heat
Full Blaze
Hot Point*
Flash of Fire*
Wild Fire
SMOKEJUMPERS
Wildfire at Dawn*
Wildfire at Larch Creek*
Wildfire on the Skagit*

Delta Force
Target Engaged*
Heart Strike*
Wild Justice*
Midnight Trust*

Emily Beale Universe Short Story Series

The Night Stalkers
The Night Stalkers Stories
The Night Stalkers CSAR
The Night Stalkers Wedding Stories
The Future Night Stalkers

Delta Force
Th Delta Force Shooters
The Delta Force Warriors

Firehawks
The Firehawks Lookouts
The Firehawks Hotshots
The Firebirds

White House Protection Force
Stories

Future Night Stalkers
Stories (Science Fiction)

SIGN UP FOR M. L. BUCHMAN'S NEWSLETTER TODAY

and receive:
Release News
Free Short Stories
a Free Book

Get your free book today. Do it now.
free-book.mlbuchman.com

Printed in Great Britain
by Amazon